# The Sermons of Reverend Smith

## Nathan Isbourne

Nathan Isbourne
23/09/19

*For Peace*

**Also by Nathan Isbourne**

*The Place Between Two Heart Beats*
*Soldier Tom: A Hundred Years On*

Wasn't there a time
When a song we used to sing
Of perfection of our love,
A vow to paths of peace?

Wasn't there an hour
When a treaty we did make
To end all wars and suffering,
When hostilities surely ceased?

Wasn't there a day
When church bells rang aloud,
When soldiers laid their weapons down,
Returning home at last?

Wasn't there a mass
With desire contained in fervent prayer
To reclothe us in our rightful minds,
To forgive our foolish ways?

And isn't there a land
We've heard of long ago,
Obliged to render hope,
In peace its glory find?

*To all who hold out their hands in peace,*
*to peace lovers, peace writers and peace talkers,*
*to peace singers and peace makers.*

# Prologue

In Nathan Isbourne's previous work 'Soldier Tom', the narrator of the story was 'Peace'. In this work however, Peace, portrayed as an Eastern entity, has become one of the main protagonists who enters into an unusual dialogue with a Western Christian minister. As you can imagine, the conflicts in perception that arise are profound. Through this story, Isbourne, in his own imaginative and fanciful style, tries to bridge unnecessary but naturally occurring gaps in inter-religious understanding and brings the reader, perhaps, into a challenging inquiry of the limitations and veracity of their own perceptions and beliefs.

It is hoped this work will encourage the reader to talk with courtesy and with goodwill with peoples of all faiths, or none, about the immense and grave problems that affect all of us in today's world. It asks relevant, thought-provoking and difficult questions, yet is in no way written to cause anyone any offense.

As with his previous works, this work also asks if we are ready to live in a way which would bring about a world of very diverse yet very fallible human beings who have the means to live in humility towards one another, show respect to one another and safeguard the peace and well-being of one another.

The peace that we have known, the diversity of culture that is ours, the message of acceptance and tolerance of other faiths that do us proud, that are indeed part of us, need to be protected and strengthened, not diminished by fear and misunderstanding. By the will of God, *insha'Allah*, and by the work of Man, this will be so and there will be peace.

- *Peace, for the 7th July 2019*

# THE SERMONS OF REVEREND SMITH

Reverend Smith was loved,
Reverend Smith was admired,
Reverend Smith uplifted and inspired
The congregation in his church.
His voice was strong,
His stature tall,
His back was straight,
He showed no compromise,
But took the Word
From which he never veered
And threw it out,
And captured hearts and minds.
He pleased his flock, expanded it,
Was headed for the top.
He knew his Book, inside out,
Was quick to yield a verse or two,
Prescribe a Psalm or Song,
Exactly what was needed
For those who needed God.
His prayers brought tears,

His insights more,
His Bible knowledge was profound,
His faith was never in any doubt,
He was a credit to his Lord.

He loved his wife, and she loved him,
Their life was all it could be,
They were fulfilled,
They were envied
For the happiness they showed.
They were each other's confidant,
There were no secrets to keep hidden,
Their trust in the goodness of each other
Went beyond their imperfections.
She stood by his side, supported him,
And his ear heard her advice,
For his vocation could not be ministered
Without a woman's voice.
And when time was short and requests piled up
They divided up the tasks,
For only a man and a woman
Could do all the things God asked.

His days were filled with service,
His nights were full of dreams
That helped him in his mission
That led him on his path.
They were always worth the effort
Of recalling and reviewing
For often they shed light on

Something yet unseen.
His dream that night was vivid,
Stayed with him all day,
"I'm sending you a visitor," it said,
"I know you'll host him well,
I know you'll give him freedom
To say that which he will.
I know you'll give him liberty
To talk in his own tongue,
And I hope that you won't question
The reason he chose you."

He explained it to his wife
Who he'd woken up at dawn
And they wondered who the visitor was
Though welcome he would be,
Though the Reverend wondered also
Why the dream had 'hoped' in him
When his faith and obedience to his Lord
Had never shown exception,
Had never wavered, never faltered,
Never been in question.
But he had work to do
And couldn't fall asleep
So he started Sunday's sermon early
Then got on with his daily tasks
Of visiting those with sickness,
Of organising Christenings,
Rehearsing weddings
And lunching with the deacons,

Then spending time in the southern chapel
To reflect in reverence.

It was here he was aware
Of someone close behind him,
But he looked around and wondered why
No-one could be seen.
It felt a little eerie,
And made him quite uneasy,
But he shrugged it off and whispered,
"I'm under God's protection."
He descended on the kneeler
And placed his hands together,
He closed his eyes and said a prayer,
But the feeling reappeared.
He became a child at midnight
Where the darkness held a bump
And held his breath and knelt quite still
In hope it would disappear.
Then he heard the movement
Of a person to his right
And with the utmost courage
Managed to open his eyes.

"By God!" he almost shouted.
"Who the heck are you?"
And found himself involuntarily
Jumping to the side,
Scrambling on his palms and soles
Till his back hit panelling

From where he watched the apparition,
Though in truth it looked so real.
It raised its head up from the floor
And knelt like him in prayer,
Its scarf fell from its head,
He saw its features clear:
A man with swarthy skin
And a neatly trimmed white beard.
The Reverend kept looking,
His mouth now quite agape,
He had no problem with the Holy Spirit,
But not a full-fledged ghost.
Again with garnered courage
He stuttered out a word:
"Who…, who…, who are you?"
"Ismi Salam," it said.
"What?" inquired the Reverend
Even more perplexed,
"Ismi, ismi, what was that?"
As it turned to look at him.

*"Ismi Salam, ismi Salam, ismi Salam*," it said.
"My name is Peace.
When your mouth is dry,
When your stomach's empty,
When your hope is lost,
Is faltering, is absent,
My name is Peace, I am Peace.
I come to you in peace,
In the air you breathe,

In the words I say,
In thoughts that appear,
My name is Peace.

*"As-Salam Aleykum,* may peace be with you,
Is a greeting that I mean.
I flow between the pews of churches,
Rise from carpet lines in mosques,
Pervade synagogues and temples,
I knock on every door each day,
My name is Peace.
Good day, good morning, hello,
May peace be with you,
This is my name,
Let me stay, let me stay,
Invite me in if I am not already there.
When anger comes my name is Peace,
When sadness cries and hearts are closed
I do not leave, I'm always there,
A gentle breeze upon your face,
A whisper in your ear,
My name is Peace, my name is Peace,
*Ismi Salam.*

"When paths divide
My name is on each signpost
Pointing in both ways.
When differences arise,
When disagreements come,
I call on peaceful means.

If one feels right and one feels wrong
It is of no care to me,
For what is right for one
For another can be wrong.
But understand their needs,
Understand their ways,
I do not ignore a solitary tear,
I see all fear, feel all the pain,
But still my name is Peace.

*"Wa Aleykum Salam* my friend,
My name is Peace, my name is Peace,
*Ismi Salam.*
I come in peace,
I have no gun,
Let me enter, do not run,
I come only with the message:
There will be peace,
There will be peace.
My name is not distress,
Nor discontent, nor hatred,
Nor war, nor revenge,
It is Peace, it is Peace and only Peace.
I believe I've seen the heart of God,
From here I see more things,
From here I see God's joys and pains,
From *Allah*, Yahweh, God or Cause,
*Ar-Rahman, Ar-Raheem,*
*As-Salam*, Peace,
And only Peace is my name."

And then it faded into nothing,
As if nothing had been there,
And the Reverend heard his continued pleas
To his Lord, the Word and Blood,
Muttering as if a giant chain
Was pulling him to Hell,
With a heart that seemed to wish
To thump out from his chest,
And lungs that seemed to hinder
His need for renewed breath.
He had no idea of the time,
He huddled in the corner,
When his wife came in quite worried
Searching for her husband,
And turned the chapel light on
To see his feeble stature,
To see his distant stare,
To see his hunching posture,
To see his blatant fear.
She too was alarmed
And asked him what was wrong,
But got no more than mumblings
So got him to his feet
And helped him to relearn to walk
To take him home and sit him down,
To make a cup of tea,
But it remained untouched
And grew quite cold
Well into the evening.

She helped him into bed,
He curled into a ball,
He didn't even pray before
She covered him in sheets.
She sat beside his shivering,
But couldn't feel a fever,
Hearing incoherent repetitions
Of one or two foreign words.
Was he speaking tongues,
Was he deep in trance,
Should she call the doctor
Or let him rest and sleep?
She spooned him and caressed him,
Stroked him like a child,
Calling on their Heavenly Father
To help him through this trial.
But it was well into the night
When his breath became nocturnal
And his voice that was so unlike his own
Quietened and stalled.

In the morning he lay still,
Untroubled in his slumber,
She didn't want to break his peace
So cancelled his appointments.
She made excuses for his absence,
Told everyone not to worry,
It was only a twenty-four hour thing,
He'd soon be fully recovered.
But she continued praying for his well-being

Until his eyes were open,
And he smiled obliviously at her face
Then jolted as he remembered.
"What was it dear?" she asked,
His hand within her hands,
"I thought you'd seen the Devil,
But you'd have soon have chased him off."

With time he sat up straight,
Cushioned by his pillows,
And trying to make some sense of things
He confided in his wife.
"I believe the visitor came," he said,
"And then he disappeared,
Right before my very eyes
He vanished like a fading wind,
Though a tornado in my thoughts.
It was a ghost for sure,
But a ghost I could have touched,
And it touched me very deeply,
Deep into my soul.
Honestly it scared me,
Scared me to the core,
But when I think of the words it said,
It only talked of peace.
And when I think a little more,
Its name was Peace and only Peace,
*Ismi Salam*, it said.
And only when I recalled the dream,
I perceived how it saw God,

But thought such things were reserved for saints,
Not for common vicars,
And it was far from what a normal visitor is,
Someone in need of succour."

Within a little time
The Reverend regained strength,
He regained confidence and took a pen
To write what he had heard,
For everything he'd heard
Was etched upon his mind,
Was solid in his consciousness
And rang like Sunday's bells.
He took to pottering about
Then getting back to normal,
But it was clear to his wife his mind remained
Far from that before him,
And it was clear to those who came and went
He was somewhat absent-minded,
And to others it was somewhat bizarre
That he walked around in slippers.
But within another day or two
All seemed almost usual
And the event that had occurred before
Seemed less and less supernatural.
And they thought that that was that,
That the visitor had gone,
That he'd said his peace and bid farewell,
Had done what he had come for,
So the Reverend opened up his notebook

To finish off his sermon
From words contained within the Word,
From commentaries on his doctrine,
From hymns and prayers from the common books,
From what parishioners asked him,
And apart from the vestige of an inkling
This shepherd returned to flocking.

When Saturday came all was prepared,
It was business back to normal,
But when Sunday formed its early morn
That vestige reappeared, niggled him awake,
The inkling kept his mind alert,
Then spoke to him in words unheard
Except between his ears,
And made him rise to take up pen,
Sitting at his desk.

"When the day is young," it said,
"In the dark before the dawn,
When the night is silent
And the birds have not yet flown,
I call upon my brother,
I need a hand to write,
He wakes and hears my bidding
And opens up his mind.
He doesn't know what he will hear,
But waits with pen and ink,
He is my voice, he is my link,
I need to make things clear.

I don't believe it's written
On paper, stone or lead,
That the horrors that I see each day
Are prearranged by God:
A child laid out upon a beach,
Its face hid in the sand,
A child hid under blood and dust
With murder all around,
A father holding limply
His son who lives no more,
A mother crying desperately
Falling to the floor.
God is not a monster,
He does not plan such ills,
It is with greatest agony
He sees these daily things:
A boy with all his skin burnt off,
A girl who's lost her face,
A student on a classroom wall,
A baby hung upon a fence.
He's not the cause of this,
How could this be his Will,
His ways are ways of endless love,
His paths are paths of peace.

"His servant wear's a cross,
But too the crescent moon,
He wears a Buddhist robe,
A *gutra* and a *thobe*:
How brightly shine his colours

Like Joseph's multi-coloured cloak.
Every door he's stepped through
Has added to its sheen,
Nothing has been tarnished,
But polished bright and clean.
His mind and heart have grown
Through many years of voyage,
His mind is broad and wide,
His heart embraces all.

"His servant's travelled many lands,
He speaks with many tongues,
He no longer has the ignorance
And prejudice of youth,
He knows his faults, regrets his errors,
But has gained humility instead,
And has reason to be grateful
For the friends that he has made.

"To those He gives the task
To set the record straight,
To remind us of the one great truth
That is so often buried deep
Under mountains of interpretation,
Under piles of commentary,
It is the one great Constant,
The first of all the bricks.
God gave it to Confucius,
God gave it to the Jews,
You'll find it in the Buddhist script,

In the Gospels and Hadith too.
It has never changed, and it never will,
It's been there from the very start,
Written with the earliest quill.
It is the very pinnacle
Of each and every faith,
It is the true foundation stone,
The root of faith itself.
It's the axiom at the centre
Of a man of God, of a man of peace,
That leaves only one interpretation,
That drives the wheels of peace.

'Love thy neighbour as thyself',
Underline it in your Books,
 'Do not do unto others
What you wouldn't do to self'.
Put this in your pocket,
Keep room within your heart,
Hold on to it with all your strength,
This is your way of life.
It's the North Star in the north,
The rudder that is true,
The penny on the pendulum
That keeps the clock on time.

"So if you love your God
With all your heart and soul,
Let your heart and mind be strong,
Love your fellowman.

Do not falter, do not waver
Wherever you may be,
Offer kindness, offer friendship,
Then kindness will return.

"God's world is a land of many
Living side by side
Who believe in peace and tolerance,
Are totally colour blind,
Who look at each and every faith
With moderation and respect,
Who are loyal to the Human Rights
Of each and every man,
Who share all land as if one band,
As brothers bound by birth,
For when the truth be told,
And when the truth be known,
One united common humanity
Is there within our sights.
This is as I see things,
This is my belief."

It was a different sermon
To that which he had written,
Though undoubtedly contained
Both common sense and reason,
Yet also spoke in ways
In which his Church might disapprove,
And if he spoke of different creeds
Parishioners would be confused.
Yet the visitor came to him,
Was a voice that would be heard,
What was he to make of it?
The stress was quite absurd.

In the end he chose to clear his mind
So he could do his job,
To feed, uplift and satisfy
Those sat before him in the pews.
He climbed up to the pulpit,
He opened up his Book,
He turned to One Corinthians
Then Luke and John and Mark,
But paused between two verses
As he eyed his rank and file,
For the visitor was now standing
In the middle of the aisle.

His pause paused on for longer
Till folk began to wonder
What it was that made him stare
At the emptiness above cold flagstones,

Till whispers turned to murmurs
And the verger coughed and psst
To catch the attention of the Reverend
Who was in a pickled mix,
To bring him back onto the track
Of the sermon he'd prepared,
To help him to continue to
Evangelise and save.
The verger climbed the pulpit steps
And tugged upon his surplice,
Then pulled as if a bell rope
And the Reverend almost fell,
But at least regained his senses
To focus on his aid.
He then gazed on the holy pages
Not daring to look up
And read a few more lines of Scripture
In intermittent spurts,
But the visitor drew closer,
Stood right there at his side,
Captured back his attention,
So close he came they could have shared
Each other's shoes and station.

"*Ism Salam, ismi Salam*," the Reverend said,
Although his throat was choked.
"My name is Peace, my name is Peace,"
He uttered half in trance,
But so peculiar was the feeling,
He fought as in a nightmare,

Then yelled, "I can't! I can't, not yet!"
And the visitor withdrew.
The Reverend stood there panting,
Sweat falling from his brow,
He swayed and held on to the rail,
Till the verger helped him down
And the organist pulled out knobs
And pressed down on his ivory
And the congregation sang another hymn
To praise the One they loved.

*****

The Reverend dawdled in the vestry,
He hid behind its door,
Imagining the gossiping
Between the tea and homemade scones.
He placed his head between his hands,
Looked down between his feet,
He'd had dominion over his life,
But now life had dominion over him.
Again his wife came to the rescue,
Was a trusted ear in which to speak,
But still he fumbled with his words
To explain events not understood.
She held his hand, she gave him time,
He admired her graceful patience,
"He came again, the visitor,
He tried to speak through me," he said.
"Did you see him walk the aisle?" he asked,

But she only shook her head.
"He's coming back, soon I think,
And he won't be leaving soon,
But I fear that which he wants to say
Even if it's in goodwill.
I think he is an Easterner,
Though peace be universal,
And I feel his soul is very old,
And his truth is far beyond my own,
Encompasses far more,
And I don't know how the way he speaks
Will be received by all our friends.
But I guess I must be willing
To host this guest we're given,
Though he may not be invited,
He's definitely staying with us.
I presume that providence knows,
Why he's chosen me,
So I presume as well I should be able
To lend my voice to his."

They ventured for a walk
Along the country lanes
And climbed a while upon the hill
That rose above the village
For clean, fresh air, for new perspective,
For nature's calming song,
But the Reverend only saw his church spire
Rise above the houses
And worried for his ministry,

Worried for his job,
For his job was to say what the Church wished said
Not what Peace insisted,
And though the East held the Holy Land
It also held him ransom
For he'd have to empty out his mind
And maybe too his body
To let Peace inside with freedom,
To give to Peace its chance.
But it was a lovely day he thought,
And he loved his lovely wife
So in the end it would end all right
And would certainly be a venture,
And for whatever happened
There would be reason
And that reason could be peace.
So prepared he was, come what may
To let the visitor in
When next he came, when next he knocked
He'd open up his mind.

When Wednesday came he strolled along
Guided by the church bells,
It was the evening practice group
Hanging from the cables.
It was also Bible study night,
A circle of devotion,
Devoted fellow Christians
Learning who their God was.

The circle was embedded
Within the Word of God,
Turning holy pages
And reading verse aloud,
Being moved and being educated,
Being filled emotionally,
Parishioners holding their Book with awe,
Reading through its stories,
Its parables, psalms and gospels,
Imbuing and discussing
The meanings held in the narrow print
Upon the gilt edges pages,
Parishioners totally unaware
Of what would happen next.

It was deep within Ephesians
As Paul spoke to the faithful
When the Reverend knew the time was now
That his voice would be of use to
The figure standing distantly,
But edging ever closer,
To the figure knowing what to say,
Though the Reverend was no wiser.
He closed his eyes and inhaled deeply,
Calmed his anxious flesh
Then drifted off as if to sleep
And let the visitor speak.

"I hear bells aside *Al-Adhan* sound,
*Al-Fatiha* from the pulpit read,

'Our Father who art in Heaven'
In a mosque be said,
'Lord and Father of Mankind'
In a mosque be sung.
I see one prostrate beside
One who humbly kneels,
The *Qu'ran* beside the Bible sit,
And *Suraat* read between the hymns.
With this I can believe
The world is coming closer:
Behold the possibilities of tolerance,
The possibility to understand,
Behold the possibilities through dialogue,
The possibilities in peace.

"I'm happy to hear bells ringing
From atop a minaret,
I'm happy to hear *Al-Fatiha*
Read within a church,
I'm happy to hear the laughter
Of a Muslim child
Within a Christian home,
I'm happy to hear the greetings
Of any man to any other soul.
Love cannot be limited
To only those you're told to love,
Love is not confined
To the limits of one group,
Love is free to everyone,
So let your hand shake every hand,

And don't let love be denied,
By bigotry and lies.

"You may not worship as another does
And he may not worship as you do,
But to him please say these words:
I will not place you lower,
I will not judge your way,
I will not think the less of you,
My brother you are still.
I will not think ill thoughts of you,
I will not cite in hate,
I will not feel superior,
My hand is there to shake.
Your life is just as sacred,
Your friendship just as dear,
Let me approach with open arms
For I wish to kiss your cheek.

"I believe a servant speaks,
Of different ways to peace,
And then again and then again
Of peace, of peace, for peace.
He does not shoot a bullet,
He does not drop a bomb,
He does not lie or use deceit,
He does not storm a holy shrine.
And as you hear these verses
I hope that you agree,
There is not a single word

That does not call for peace,
Though it may be said in stranger ways
Than which your ears find common,
For my name is Peace, *ismi Salam*,
And peace is my desire,
For I wish nothing else but peace
And beg for peace around the world
By purely peaceful means.
This is how I see things,
This is my belief."

The faces of the fellowship
Stared squarely at the Reverend,
The mouths that hung agape
Closed slowly at the interruption.
They were surprised and shocked
At the Reverend's voice
That sounded like a newcomer,
Was not the Reverend's own,
And definitely wasn't in anyway similar
To the way he usually spoke.

Although his eyes had closed,
His face showed animation,
He'd sat erect and rigid
As the words came clearly out
Loud and clear and adamant
With the confidence of conviction,
But now the voice had faded
And the Reverend's head bowed down,
Upon his chest it rested
As if his soul had just departed,
As if he sat there empty,
As if a vessel voided,
So glad they were to see his ribs
Rising up then falling,
And glad they were to hear his breath
Whistling sleep between his lips.

Perplexed, confused, concerned,
One tapped him on the shoulder

Then nudged him and then shook him
Till his eyelids lifted and pupils focused,
Bemused at all the fussing faces
Facing all his way,
Exhausted by what must have happened,
Though he recollected nought,
Nought except he'd been possessed
In a purely benevolent fashion,
That he'd given his body to another
And the other had worn him out.

He couldn't answer questions,
He couldn't explain the why,
He could only trust in God
Who worked in mysterious ways,
And asked for a glass of water,
For his throat was rather parched,
And asked for them to tell him
What it was he'd said,
And found that though the content
Was religious in its nature,
It crossed accepted doctrinal lines,
Had gone beyond what he'd expected,
And with no need for reflection
He knew there would be consequences,
For he knew his flock's perceptions,
And knew that tongues would wag.

\*\*\*\*\*

His wife let him sleep late,
She didn't set the alarm
So he woke to the smell of eggs and toast
Instead of jingling bells.
He laid a while in bed
Pondering on his circumstances
Then rose to wash and don his clothes
And clip on his dog collar.
She raised an eye on seeing him,
Boy how quick news travels,
And kissed him tenderly on the cheek
To assuage his present travails.
"Did the visitor call again?" she asked
As she dished him up his food,
He nodded and he shrugged his shoulders,
Then sighed before he broke the yoke.

The land line rang, on the hour,
The office had just opened,
And the first call made was from the Bishop
Who was now within the loop.
"My friend," he said. "My dear, dear friend,
What is this I've been hearing?
Quranic messages, talk of mosques,
That's not what you are paid for.
Keep things simple, keep to the script,
We use the Holy Scripture,
Do you need a few days off?
This work can be quite stressful.
You won't be the first to take a break,

Our retreat is very beautiful,
But whatever you do, don't disappoint,
You are the village shepherd,
We have great hopes,
You've always shone,
You're soon to be promoted.
Look my boy, I'm pretty busy,
I'll slot you in quite soon,
We need to talk, face to face,
You're part of God's great plan!"

And, apart from parting platitudes,
The Reverend said no more,
He didn't insist, he didn't relate
More than the Bishop wanted to hear.
Not only was he spellbound,
He was curious about the visitor,
In fact he couldn't deny to himself
That he wished to meet him more,
And he found that he was drawn to know
More about his origins,
For although he was well-acquainted
With the tenets of Judaism,
He remained ashamedly ignorant
Of the teachings of Islam,
Which he presumed would somewhat mirror
What had come before,
And assumed would offer challenges
For the differences it bore.

The week passed by quite slowly
He had more time on his hands,
The telephone didn't ring as often
And the knocker knocked far less.
He knew that folk were shying
Away from what seemed strange,
And the strange was often frightening
And unfortunately it was him.
But still the core stayed loyal,
The compassionate showed compassion,
And the patient attended patiently,
While the elders showed experience
And friendship stayed with friends,
And indeed news got around
So the inquisitive inquired,
And when Sunday came the pews were full
Of many irregular guests
Who hoped perhaps for a spectacle,
Or a juicy talking point.

They sang the hymns,
The rafters raised,
The collection boxes rattled,
Prayers were prayed and readings read
Then all went silent for the sermon.
Even coughs were held in check
And sniffles snuffled out
As the Reverend climbed into the pulpit
With no notebook in his hand,
For the only thing he felt he needed

Was a chair on which to sit,
And hidden down beside his feet
A recorder with a fresh cassette.
"Please forgive this change in tack," he said.
"Today things will be different.
In fact, I don't know what I'll say,
But believe someone has prepared a speech.
I believe it will be something
Unlike the usual fare,
But even so I believe it will
Be something to inspire
And something to discuss,
And something centred on the will for peace,
For peace and only peace."

Once again he closed his eyes,
He readied for the presence,
The world went dark, the visitor approached
In the clarity of his mind's eye.
Then once again his soul was taken
And his companion moved right in
To speak in its accustomed way
With its unaccustomed voice.

"Despite the rituals of your faiths,
Despite the customs of your lands,
Despite the robes that cover skin,
Despite the cloth that veils a face,
The eyes uphold the greater truth.

"Revealed are needs and weaknesses,
Unfurled are fears and strengths,
Curiosities and sympathies peer out
With attractions and disgusts,
And manifest are indifference,
Manifest are loves and hates.

"Nothing can be hidden,
Neither sorrow, indignity nor joy,
For everything is clear,
The truth is always there:
The humanness of life,
Where instinct creates feelings,
The freedom in one's thinking,
Despite the written rules.
You can't deny you're human first,
Before beliefs that are professed,
Though culture and tradition
Affect the way you act,
Your common human quality
Remains the binding fact.

"By all means do surrender,
Surrender unto God,
But remember you are human
And humans have their faults.
If you give yourself completely
Give yourself to peace,
For I believe that God
Is peace and God is love,

These are the only paths,
Though one man may claim one thing
And another claim another,
Unless he's proved he's of peace and love
To him do not surrender.
Do not give him your mind,
Do not give him your heart,
And don't be swayed by others
Who before you he swayed first.
Do not choose a side,
For to choose is to divide,
And there are no divisions
In a family at peace, in a family of love
That's lovingly bound and tied.

"By the name of the morning star
No soul is all alone,
But has a guardian over it,
Assigned by God to watch and guide,
From where it is and what it knows
Towards its destination,
Which in the end and ultimately
Is the same as yours.
So know despite your worries,
Know despite your words,
A man is led within God's care
Before and past his youth,
And his final breath will see
A very different soul
Shaped by experience and visions

Throughout his earthly years.
So do not feel obliged
To shunt him left or right,
Suffice to help him listen,
Suffice to help him hear
His guardian in the quiet hours
Of his day and of his night.

"And that child of yours is my child,
Your concern for him is mine,
For his safety and his well-being,
His success, his hopes, and fears.
I only see a child,
I do not see a Muslim,
A Christian or a Jew,
I rejoice with you, *masha'Allah,*
For his health and dreams and joy.

"Introduce him to a foreign child
With brown eyes and black hair,
So he may grow accustomed to
Your child's blue eyes and skin that's fair.
Say 'This child is your brother
From another land,
Converse and learn from him,
Take him by the hand.'
Take opportunity to show
He is a welcome friend
Before someone convinces him
That they are deadly fiends.

Give them understanding
Instead of war and death,
Show them what love and respect are,
Bequeath to them a world of peace.

"I am a voice that does not change,
When changes come I stand my ground.
Not one letter hesitates,
Not one syllable quivers,
Not before and still not now,
I was before and I am now,
I will be there when you have gone
And there when others come,
The past, the present and the future
Are suffused with peaceful words.

"I am in the light, and I am in the air,
I am in the darkness, and I am in the void,
And I am in the quiet mind
That allows me there to dwell.
You can hear me, you can feel me,
And you can understand me,
And you will surely see me
In the goodwill and good deeds
Of good men.

"I am here for I believe
The world that now exists
Is not the world God had within
His heart nor in His head:

It's rupturing and fragmenting,
Its genocides are astounding,
Its horrors are appalling,
It's led by those misled.

"I am here to open minds,
To turn dark hearts
Away from crimes.
Far from the paths of peace
Some men are full of hate,
Far from humane paths
That are mindful of the Human Race.

"I am here to request you think
That the Day will only come
Not by the Will of God
But the ignorance of men.
The earth has been created
As home and hearth for kin,
It cannot be within His plan
To see it all condemned?

"I ask for common sense,
I ask for common good,
There's room for all God's peoples
Created out of love.
I ask you reconcile beliefs
That may profoundly differ,
To build bridges across borders
As friends without agendas.

"I see you wipe your tears,
Know the things that you are feeling,
Your belly full of earthly years,
Disasters that are numbing.
But once again I ask,
Do not think this is His Will:
How can he will for pain?
And do not think that it is written
That tomorrow will bring ill
For this is fatalistic
And discourages any change,
Change that Man must bring
If there's any hope for peace.

"I don't think God differentiates
One's posture when in fear:
A man prostrate, a man on knees,
He places none above the other,
He hears the language of the heart,
He's there to offer succour.
So do not think your way is right,
Your rituals are the best,
God watches men while in the street,
Even those who don't believe.

"And I ask you too to think
That as the Parent of all men,
God does not feel your suffering,
He is in no way blind?
And have you ever thought

That as the Creator of the world,
God does not worry fitfully
For the future of mankind?
Have you ever wondered,
I mean 'really' understood,
That the blood He put within your veins,
He put in every man?
He hears you call Him many things,
Revere Him with high names,
But do you know the fact of it,
That He is Suffering?
His heart bleeds in a way
You cannot comprehend,
His head is heavy with dismay
By fighting without end?

"You suffer in yourself,
Your family and your friends,
But He suffers for ten billion,
For each woman, man and child.
This is how I see things,
This is my belief."

When the Reverend finally woke
The organ pipes were blowing,
Deep and sonorous vibrations wove
Through the church's rood screen,
And the congregation sang
A familiar song they loved.
But rubbing his eyes to clear his sight
He saw seats prematurely empty,
Familiar faces gone,
Heard choristers whisper between the verses
While pulling distracted faces.
Then standing at the door
To shake parishioners' hands
Praise was somewhat limited,
Thanks were left ungiven,
And silence replaced comments
And comments were reserved,
But those closest lingered longest
With their trusted friend,
To ask of the uncharacteristic nature
Though got little in response,
But even these he knew would struggle
For their world was in the Word,
Yet he tried to explain as best he could,
To alleviate concern,
But could see a split developing
That he didn't know how to bridge.

When nestled in the Rectory
In the quiet of his study

He pressed 'play' to listen intently
To the message on the tape.
He listened then rewound,
He listened two more times,
Wishing to find answers
To what it was he heard,
But the more times that he listened,
The more questions that he had,
And knew the quest to unravel this
Would be a Gordian knot,
Would take perhaps his lifetime
And then perhaps some more.

The knot was truly tangled,
Was knitted in tight knots,
And the only way to approach the quandary
Was with an open mind and heart,
Was with willingness to accept another
And the way he lived his life,
Where respect for tradition and love for Prophet
Were just as strong as his,
And were not to be dismantled,
Were not to be dismissed,
But needed understanding
To know why squabbles start,
To know why Peace was visiting,
To build the bridge to peace.

\*\*\*\*\*

As was to be expected
The telephone rang at nine,
It was the Bishop's secretary,
An appointment had been made.
He had to face the music,
Be lectured on his trade,
So he drove up to the cathedral,
His tail between his legs,
And parked beside the cloisters
Then took a long deep breath.
"I understand your troubles,"
The Bishop started out.
"You're not the first to lapse a little,
Start thinking for yourself,
But we are the Church of England,
Do things the English way,
And for sure we're very spiritual,
Have a few saints of our own,
But one shouldn't act like a Spiritualist
And let the dead speak out.
Our ways are close to heart,
Our rituals set out straight,
Are what parishioners expect from us,
There's no need to detract, no need to disturb
The attachment to our religion
That is bound by common creed.
There's no need to breed doubt,
No need to broaden minds,
No need to encourage thought
Beyond a reasonable range.

Please don't get me wrong,
You are an intelligent man,
You have my upmost sympathy,
But when your mind goes out of bounds
Please keep your thoughts inside,
And if your visitor returns once more
Please usher him aside.
I'm sending you to Wycliffe Hall
For a short refresher course,
Chat with the teachers while you're there,
Discuss reasons for our past,
Debate with those adept at reason
To reason all things out,
Then if you have a moment,
But only if you do,
Look into the library
At comparative religious thought,
For perhaps there truly will be
For you a change in tack,
Perhaps your vocation needs updating
For each horse has its course,
But please don't see a villain
When you look at me,
It's long since now I was a novice,
My experience is profound."

*****

Wycliffe Hall was grand,
Wycliffe Hall was old,

It stood amongst the hallowed colleges
Between Oxford's thousand spires.
It was an epicentre
Of his Church's heart and mind,
He was honoured and inspired
To step into its grounds.
Steeped in great tradition,
It smelt of aged text,
Its aura promised knowledge
And offered greater depth.
So he stepped across its threshold
With great expectancy
Was infused with respect and awe
While searching for more meaning.

Everyone was helpful,
Everyone was kind,
The minds that he conversed with
Were undoubtedly in their prime.
There were traditionalists and modernists
Who had discussions of their own,
Conservatives and progressives
Whose logics were renowned.
Each thought wove a different strand
Yielding opposite conclusions,
But he was drawn to mysticism
And talked more with the readers
Of things beyond parochial scope,
Tucked underneath the edges.
From these he garnered curious looks

While explaining his dilemma,
But also gathered pointers
And lists of reference books:
Names of pertinent authors,
Of subject matter experts.
And while he sat with one mind
Another walked on in,
The visitor dropped in unannounced,
As he usually did,
But this time didn't enter him,
But stopped short so the Reverend
Could hear the things he said
And let the Reverend speak for him
While consciously awake,
Of things clothed in another religion,
Birthed in another culture,
But relevant and timely,
And pertinent to all. He said:

"How do you convince a man
Who was born in war and lives through war,
Who has never questioned the norms he knows,
For whom peace is not envisioned,
Cannot be explained,
For the word itself isn't understood,
Is abnormal in itself,
Is counter to the way he thinks?

"How do you convince a man
Who was schooled and lives in hate

Of the error of his perceptions,
The inadequacy of his thoughts,
That the actions of his life
Perpetuate the tears,
Delay the day when peace will come,
When children have careers?

"How do you convince a man
Who's lost all that he has loved
That he's not a fool for trying
To forget and to forgive,
That revenge, though be it sweet,
Will bring a bitter end,
That through a will for reconciliation
There actually will be peace?

"Jews await the First One,
Christians, they have Jesus,
Muslims have their Second Coming,
Others have their Babas,
But who is this Messiah
That God still desperately yearns for?
He is the messiah in each man,
Not only in just one,
He is an act of kindness,
He is a lesson learnt,
He is in all human beings
Waiting to be used.
He is a helping hand
That pulls another to his feet,

He is a divining rod
That leads only towards love,
He is a compass point
That only points to peace.
He is not to be awaited,
He's not to be looked for,
He's in each and every one of us,
Not just only one.
Just one man will not bring peace,
Everyone is called,
It's the messiah in each and all of us
That is the Messiah we all need.
This is as I see things,
This is my belief.

"Indeed,
What is the religion that was ordained to Noah,
That was commended to Abraham, Moses and Jesus,
That was inspired in us,
To establish and be not divided therein,
To argue not between ourselves?
But yet there are those that do,
Who allow prejudice to betray them,
Bigotry to blind them,
Arrogance to defeat them,
And insularity to confine them.

"What is the religion that was ordained,
That was commended and was inspired?
I say again, again and again,

It is to 'love one another
As you would be loved yourself,
To not do unto others
What you wouldn't have done to yourself.'
In short it is to love,
In short it is to live in peace.
This is the greatest of all God's signs,
All His requests and all His commands,
To see this in all other men,
To see this in yourself.
This is my belief.

"So men of knowledge, chosen men,
Men of knowledge, chosen men!
You know that of God's signs
Are the differences in tongues,
And the differences in skins,
Yet still I hear some scoff,
Still I hear some scowl,
Still I see some take these signs,
As reason to belittle.

"Oh how small their minds,
Oh how small their hearts,
Oh how little they have learnt,
Though they may have memorised Books.
I hear them snigger behind his back,
Even to his face,
But who was it who gave him colour,
Put the blood within his veins?

Yes, *Allah*, God, Yahweh!
So who is right and who is wrong,
Do they even think?
Years and years of study,
Yet still in ignorance.
Hundreds of chapters and verses
And they yet somehow manage
To skirt humility, to neglect gratitude,
To misunderstand that peace and love
Belong to each and every man
And are the essence of God's being.
This is my belief.

"So know that when you walk
Before another man,
You walk in front of God,
You follow in His trail,
And when you look him up and down,
Your thoughts are clear to Him,
And when you look him in the eyes
God looks back at you.

"Do you think your *thobe*
Cut high above your feet,
Do you think the cross
Hanging round your neck,
Do you think the skull cap
Resting on your head
Makes you better than he is?
Then you are wrong my friend,

You are wrong again my friend,
All too wrong again.

"What lies on the surface
Is often just a crust,
What lies underneath
Is where God puts His trust,
And if peace is at the core
The surface will not ripple,
And if the surface doesn't ripple
God puts even greater trust.
This is how I see things,
This is my belief."

The Reverend was quite grateful
For this communication was less tiring
And gave the chance for him to hear
The words that he was speaking,
Words that weren't his own
Yet from him they were issuing,
Words that Peace could say
While he was ably willing.

His associate remained silent
And then he made a "Hmmm,"
For he saw within these words
Novelty in Belief.
"You say his name is Peace?" he checked,
"A visitor in a dream?
You had the dream and the dream came true,
And the visitor's from the East?
I trust in what you're saying,
Far stranger things occur,
But the way that Peace is talking
Could stir a hornet's nest.
You see his tongue's in Islam,
But he's breaking some set rules:
For one he's innovating
What one should never change,
But, as we know ourselves,
Orthodoxy needs consensus,
And as we're well aware
Consensus calls for compromise
Where opposing heads nod together

For the sake of a solid whole
And doctrine is pronounced assertively
As if its writers had never argued.

"I cannot say he's wrong
For he's calling out for peace,
But there may be quite a problem
In the way he is received.
To some he'd be a welcome breath,
To others he'd be demonic,
To some he'd be allowed free speech,
To others he'd be hushed up,
Some would at least listen,
Others would not permit that,
To some he could persist,
From others he'd have to run:
Perhaps that's why he's chosen you
To give peace half a chance.
But Peace has got to start somewhere
And it's usually with rejection,
For you know how much we resist change
Being human beings,
You know how much we get offended
And how easily we offend.
So don't expect too much,
Except to be berated,
Don't expect an easy path,
You're one persuading many,
But don't give up where peace's concerned
For God is ever patient

And supports historical perspective
Where attitudes come in ebbs and flows
And politics has its breakthroughs,
And though Peace may speak in foreign terms,
We too can learn new things."

*****

At home he struggled in,
His arms were laden down
With volume upon heavy volume,
The beginning of research.
His wife perused the titles
And in her carefree manner
Joked about her husband's faith
As if he planned conversion.
He jumped right in at one-o-one,
Soon got to one-o-two,
And page by page and bit by bit
Perceived which page Peace stood on,
And saw a mission unfolding
Beyond his cherished village,
But also saw the immensity
Of what was undertaken:
The changing of perceptions, removal of ill-will,
The acceptance of another's ways,
The prescription of goodwill,
And both finally and initially
The changing of himself.

He lost himself in books,
He lost all sense of time,
His wife took care of shepherding
Where and when she could.
He rarely left his study,
Forgot to eat his meals,
She found him in the mornings
With his head upon his desk.
He didn't wash, he didn't shave
Till she produced some soap
And reminded him that cleanliness
Would please God and herself.

His notebooks overflowed
With new thought upon new,
An intravenous drip of spirit
Raced around his veins.
But interruption had to come
As weekdays passed him by
And his wife woke him to let him know
That the day was now Sunday.
Would he use his notes?
Would he need to choose some verse?
Or would he stand up unprepared,
Would the visitor give the sermon?
Indeed that was the way it was,
Peace stood near his side,
Gave him words to say aloud
To act on his behalf and say:

"God's heart feels what's across the border,
His eyes see far beyond the wall,
His hand shakes hands across all lines,
His ears hear neighbours when they call.
God will not succour hateful voices,
He will not speak a word of ill,
He is One in many billions,
But each one is His other half.

"His world does not believe in hate,
His diction has no place for war,
He knows the world He wants to build,
It's with you not without.
He has no room within His mind
For words that separate,
He will walk side by side in peace
With whom He will, not whom you wish.

"You cannot yet convince Him,
A friend's an enemy,
Or that a so-called enemy,
Is not a friend who waits to be.
You are more alike than different,
More akin than strangers,
His language is plain and simple,
It's a smile that can be trusted.

"Are you not a human first
Displaying all the attributes a human has?
Swayed this way first and then the other

By passions and desires
Inherent in the human form,
Inspired and moved by ardent words
Felt deeply in the human heart.

"Do you not express emotions:
Laughter accompanied by tears,
Anger burning like wild fire,
Yet governed too by instinct,
Of animal needs,
Domesticated or wild?
Yes, you can show compassion,
Yet a danger you remain
If threatened or astray,
If forgetful of the laws
That let men live in peaceful ways.

"You are Muslims, Christians and Jews by name,
But underneath it all, your lives are fully human
With hearts that gives volition
And emotions that need control,
That inherently look for purpose,
Inherently look for use,
That can apprehend the similarities
In your fellow men,
That each human being mirrors
Every common man,
The least common denominator being
The common human form.

"And I ask, who might God be most pleased with:
A said believer who lies and cheats,
A man whose piety is matched
Only by his deceit,
Or a Buddhist who maintains his truth
That He inspired for good,
Or an atheist for whom
Charity is his work?

"Isn't God their only keeper?
To Him is the fairness in what they do.
If any are to judge,
Perhaps it is God and only Him?
Let them live at peace and leave them be.
You can live beside them,
Show kindness when you can,
Do not turn your back on them,
They are still your fellow men.
Invite one in your home,
Offer friendship not a lecture,
And see how the power of silence
Can do more good than harm,
Can yield the peace desired,
Can be of greater worth
Than a thousand careless holy words
Shot from a zealot's mouth,
Slung from an arrogant mind
That isn't yet intelligent enough
To know it's full of flaws,
For zealotry in any form

Is poison in the air,
And each and every breath exhaled
Contaminates the world.
He fails to see what's clear to God:
That though he's underneath
A burning lantern, burning bright,
This leaves him without question
In the darkest spot.
This is my belief.

"And if the truth be known,
The belief in just one God,
In the hands of zealous bigots
Has led to so much war,
Has led to so much death.
How can this be I ask
When God is love
And God is peace?

"Some of you won't like these words,
Who am I to speak you say,
But it is not a wrong doing
To perceive differently and inquire.
Allegiance to great Books
Is durable and strong,
But my brother tells you what he hears
From an entity called Peace.

"God does not harbour any grudge,
God does not seek revenge,

These are human frailties,
He sees these plain and clear.
He is not a master
With a whip held in his hand,
His message is just peace,
Only humans talk of war.
This is my belief.

"Indeed, don't judge one harshly
For wishing only peace,
And please don't judge him brashly
For speaking as I wish.
God does not punish your misdeeds,
The earth shakes by itself,
God doesn't wish any ill or harm,
He never made a Hell:
This is Man's invention, created by his fear.
So do not look at God,
For the source of such a place,
But when you stand before Him
His eyes will make you weep:
This will be a waiting hell
And sorrow will be deep.

"Yes, hasten in good deeds,
Invite all to do what's good,
Do all that God finds pleasing,
But do not let your faith
Prevent you from proceeding
Past the threshold of your gate,

From serving other men
Who may differ in their ways.
Help all men where you can,
Help all of those in need,
It bothers God in no way
Whatever is their peaceful creed.
If your faith prevents this
Then this is not God's way,
If your faith forbids this
This is cause for shame.

"Recall or learn the holy story
Of the Good Samaritan
Who aided a complete stranger
Lying injured on the ground
While the pious walked on by
Too busy with their prayers,
Too bigoted or too frightened,
To reach within themselves.

"This story is a Book itself,
A Book within a Book,
A simple guide for all Mankind
To aid their fellow man.
For underneath a robe
Or underneath blue jeans
God's children walk their daily lives
And want to live in peace,
And a man in tears of sadness
Needs arms to hold him tight.

"Indeed, where does a father go
When his son lays in his arms
With a bullet in his heart
For a stone held in his hand,
Objecting to the way
Someone stole his land,
Had built a concrete barrier
To stop him going home?

"Where does a mother go
When her son lies in the ground
With a flag placed on his shroud,
Beneath a graven slab
Through which she cannot reach
To stroke his hair or kiss his cheek,
On which her tears fall down
Only to evaporate?

"Where can a father go
When his son is in his dreams,
But his dreams will never be
And there's pain in even happy memories.
His future has been stolen,
The world is less a soul
That no man had the right to take
And God would never order?

"Where can a mother go
When her son's not at the table,
Yet the son of the man who pulled the trigger

Eats heartily unknowing
His father's aim was praised,
His name will not be given,
He'll be at work again tomorrow
Placing crosshairs on another.

"So come into the mosque on Friday
For God will be there inside:
But He will also be outside.
Come into the synagogue on Saturday
For God will be there inside:
But also there outside.
Come into the church on Sunday
For God will be there inside:
But He will also be outside.
He will be outside in the roads
And in the alleyways,
In the gardens and the desert,
He is pervasive like the air,
Caressing as the wind.

"And what does the blown sand whisper,
What's read between the stars,
What laughter sounds within the palms,
What voices fill the dark,
How loud becomes the silence,
How soft the shifting dunes,
How quiet need the mind become
To hear the desert tunes.

"A mosque doesn't need a dome,
A church doesn't need an aisle,
A temple is a heart that pumps
Peaceful blood through peaceful veins,
That allows the eye to see
A minaret beside a stained-glass rose,
That allows the mind to guide
Legs along a path to peace.
This is how I see things,
This is my belief."

But despite his belief that Peace spoke peace
The Reverend's pews were emptier,
The wooden planks of English oak
Bore testament to a diaspora,
And the ancient rafters above his head
Sagged leadened even further,
And though Peace had his voice,
Had his full attention,
Peace also had an audience
That was in confusion,
That also felt contusions,
That was quickly disappearing,
And even his closest stalwarts
Could not but question deeper
What indeed was happening
With their sidetracked, stricken minister.

The Reverend took to long walks,
More deep and fervent prayer,
He read and read and read again
And knowledge toiled and spoiled his sleep.
The long walks were digestion,
The quiet fields adjustment,
The woods and streams put things in order
As Peace's portrayal of his truth
Settled into place
Within the Reverend's consciousness,
Within another logic,
Until it made a little more sense
And offered him more reason.

He saw where Peace had come from,
Where he was headed for,
The borders he had crossed
Within the world of thought,
And though he did not forsake Jesus,
His Lord and greatest love,
The Reverend too was becoming disciple
To the spirit known as Peace.

At times the Reverend's mind was lost
Above the rustling leaves,
And too below the golden dust
Along the limestone trails.
So deep in thought he wandered,
He would have lost his way,
If he didn't know the nooks and crannies
That a child learns while at play.
He walked along one path
And came upon a cottage,
He knew the owner Michael well
Though he lived half like a hermit.
He had his food delivered,
Kept company with his dogs,
And rarely came to town except
To wet his whistle at the Corner,
To sup a little gossip,
To tipple on a rumour,
To banter with the best of them,
To laugh with local humour.

Their paths had crossed from time to time,
But it really was lost cause
For the hermit held strong to his beliefs
While the Reverend held to his.
But that was then and now was now
And the Reverend felt quite desperate,
So he knocked upon the crooked door
Of the man who kept much to himself,
Who preferred to live away from life
He considered vastly mismanaged,
But now who could perhaps become
The most unexpected confidant.

"Door's open," Michael rasped.
"Put it on the table.
Money's on the mantelpiece,
Watch your tender fingers."
He didn't look around
Washing dishes at the sink,
Didn't see the Reverend enter
And purvey the clutter, dust and mess,
And the mousetrap on the ledge.
The Reverend coughed a short, sharp cough
To garner his attention,
An act that was successful
And brought a surprised grin.
"Well, look what the cat's dragged in," he said
"Are you here to do more battle?
Forgotten your last thrashing?
Still saving my poor soul?"

But the Reverend's lips remained quite still,
Were reluctant to bid help,
Yet the hermit saw the Reverend was
A man a little humbler,
In need of some assistance,
Who may have turned up unannounced
Yet was a welcome guest.

He put the kettle on,
Cleaned cups with soapy fingers,
Removed old books from the comfy chair
Used the cushion as a duster.
Though living all alone
He hadn't lost his social gifts,
His intelligence gave him ample ease
To exercise his wit,
A wit he'd gained at grammar school
Before renouncing worldly ways,
Before childish laughter acquiesced
And irony seceded.

"I thought my doorstep far too black," he quipped,
"For the black hem of your cassock,
I thought my opinions far too expansive
For the conclusions you've been given,
I thought my bookshelf far too eclectic
For a doctrine and its missives,
And my Bakewell tarts far too salty
For the seasoned palate of a Bishop, even.
But here you are my Reverend friend,

Are you here to listen or talk?
I hear your sermons have taken a turn
And some think for the worse.
But I can't say if you can't speak,
And I can't listen if you can't talk,
So raise your head and lower your nose,
I don't take offense.
My door is always open,
You'll find it never locked,
You'll find that I'm a friend,
And as long as you accept my ways
We'll get along just fine.
For friendship you will see
Is stronger than Belief,
And belief in friendship beyond all else
Would put many wrongs to right."

As if along a syringe needle
The Reverend swallowed first,
And as if along a sore throat
He regurgitated as yet unordered thought.
"I, I, I, well, you see," he stuttered,
Through the turmoil of self-pity.
"We never, I mean you didn't. No,
What I'm trying to say is,
Ummm, God help me. Look,
Things are changing in my life,
In my point of view,
I had what could be called an encounter, I suppose,
It's been both inspiring and a burden too.

Is there more beyond Omega?
More to be revealed?
Is holding on to old beliefs
Beneficial or detrimental?
Is truth to be reorganised
To help the world survive?
Is orthodoxy far too rigid
For God's voice to be heard?"

"My God," the hermit said.
"Not that I believe,
You really have turned circle,
Have come to Thomas' defense,
Have taken what is sacrosanct
And turned it on its head.
Are you forming a new religion?
A cult of questioning?
If so I am your first disciple,
Or perhaps instead you're mine.
At first you'll be a curiosity,
Then you'll be just awkward,
After that you'll be a nail
To be hammered down quite flat.
Unfortunately this rural area
Has very few fishermen,
There is no Sea of Galilee
In which to throw your nets.
You'll be side-lined and neglected,
Your Parish will depart,
You'll be a martyr to your cause,

If you're not martyred first.
By God," he said.
"Not that I believe, mind you.
You're going to have some fun with this,
I hope that you're prepared.

"You know it's hard for ways to change,
The proof's in history,
Just take the great and ancient mind,
The genius of Ptolemy,
Whose ideas lasted centuries,
To question was to die,
But finally the laws of mathematics
Were better understood
And once and for all we were able
To put the Sun back in its place.
Then later we had Freud
Who some said was so great
That to question was unthinkable,
But his ideas couldn't progress
Beyond his own perceptions
Without the corrections of later thought,
Without greater thought on the subject.

"But you're dealing with religions
Defensive and entrenched,
That have insisted longest
In the merits of their cause,
And even today to question
Is to encounter risk,

Courting excommunication,
In places even worse.

"To protect themselves are limits
Beyond which you cannot go
For there is a point when questions shudder
The foundations of Belief,
Where it is deemed more appropriate
To rest loyal in your Faith,
Where an inquiring mind is asked to leave
For the 'said' benefit of the whole.
Oh how easily people
Accept everything they are told
Because God is God and He can't be wrong,
But the problem isn't the Word of God,
It's the interposed words of Man
That say disbelief is not allowed,
It's in religious rules,
That disbelief is tantamount
To disobedience and treason:
Not that I believe, mind you.
Not that I believe."

\*\*\*\*\*

Michael bid farewell, from his open door,
The visit had been short, perhaps he's come for more?
As the Reverend walked back down the track
Back down towards the furore.
Michael's words once thought as false

Now seemed to hold more truth
And made his head spin even more
As doubts uncovered revealed themselves
To hold more truth than doubt,
And truth discovered revealed itself
To countermand Belief.
Once home he slumped into his chair
Feeling sorry for himself
For life that was so simple
And was easy to explain
Was turned around and upside down,
Was inside out and too complex
To let him rest in peace.
"You need a break," his good wife said.
"A chance to get away,
A chance for thought to tumble down
Into its resting place.
Your eyes are like two pin balls,
Your head is weighted down,
You need time to digest whatever is
Rattling in your brain.
Let's pop on down to London,
Stay there overnight,
We can stay with Jane and Rupert,
Take in the West End sights.
I'll call them straight away,
Before you change your mind,
The sales are on in Oxford Street,
Be a shame to miss the chance.
A little light distraction

Is what this doctor orders,
The calendar's clear for Thursday,
Clear till Friday night,
Forget the books and journals,
The change will set you right."

So off they went to Smokey
Along the M-40,
Into the city that never tired,
And parked off Baker Street.
Their friends were overjoyed
To see them once again,
It had been too long, far too long,
Both sides apologised.
It was a casual evening
With catching up to do,
And with his dog collar left at home
The Reverend's spirit lightened.
They dined in Leicester Square
Then walked up Charing Cross,
Enjoyed Lloyd-Webber's genius
Then a smooth nightcap of Croft's,
And the off-duty Reverend had to agree
That his wife knew what was best,
So with both heads on their pillows,
Before the light was off,
He kissed her on the lips,
As tenderly as when courting.
She was surprised but happily so
And touched his bristled cheeks.

"I've lost half my flock, lost half my mind,
I may lose even more," he said.
"But I couldn't bear the nightmare
Of losing you as well.
I don't know what will happen next,
I've lost all certainty,
I can't see beyond tomorrow
And the morrows that will follow."
She smiled and said "You silly fool,
I'm your wife through good and bad,
And by the way your flock isn't lost
It's only you who's changed.
They still believe in Jesus,
They love Him with such depth,
Whether in your Church or outside,
Their love remains the same.
I married you for reasons
That have never altered,
I married you by vowing
And here I've never faltered.
You are a caring man,
A man of deep devotion,
Sincere and honest and thoughtfully kind,
I'm full of admiration.
I trust in you whatever,
Even through this trial,
For this trial will make you stronger
And probably much wiser.
What happens on Earth is natural,
But the supernatural is also nature,

Less understood and less defined of course,
But its gift is to be nurtured.
So don't worry silly thing,
I'm right beside your side,
And to tell you the truth I'm rather intrigued
By everything that's happening!"


When morning came the women shopped
As always was their plan
And Rupert went to work as usual
On the Underground,
But the Reverend hung around the house
With a schedule of his own,
He showered and prayed
And checked a book
On Muslim etiquette,
Then walked along the Boating Lake
Towards the Regent Mosque,
Where he hoped to find an open door
To form a dialogue.
He hung about the foyer,
Scanned eyes around the bookshop,
Flicked through some pamphlets and free booklets,
Would return after *jumaa* prayer.
He stepped across the threshold,
Left his shoes outside the door,
Was surprised to feel how large it felt,
As menfolk gathered there.
He sat upon the carpet
In a corner at the back

For he'd read that other faiths could enter,
Though he'd never heard it said.
He watched the accepted rituals,
Listened intently to the address,
And heard the Imam singing
A shepherd's soothing words,
But also heard a headstrong ram
Protective of its lambs,
And the fervency and imperative
Seemed mission part and parcel,
There was no letting up of authority:
Those gathered 'were' to follow,
And allegiance just like loyalty
Was to be demonstrated,
And toes along the woven line
Was to be expected.
Yet the chanting of *Qu'ranic* verse
Was melodically quite beautiful,
And as the greetings to the angels
Brought proceedings to an end
He stood as did the congregation slowly
Then once again was ushered aside
As the visitor gently stepped inside
To proffer his belief. He said:

*"Ismi Salam, ismi Salam, ismi Salam,*
My name is Peace, I come in peace,
I have lived for peace, I speak in peace,
I believe in peace, there will be peace.

*"As-Salam Aleykum,* may peace be with you,
Is the greeting that we say.
I flow between the pews of churches,
Rise from carpet lines in mosques,
Pervade synagogues and temples,
I knock on every door each day.

"When paths divide
My name is on each signpost
Pointing in both ways.
When differences arise,
When disagreements come,
I call on peaceful means.
I have no gun,
I come only with the message:
There will be peace,
There will be peace.

"My friends, my friends, my dear, dear brothers
I ask for you to listen, to my point of view
That time has shaped and altered,
To what I believe is truth.
I believe I've seen the heart of Allah,
From there I saw more things,
From there I saw God's joys and pains,
From Allah, Yahweh, God or Cause,
*Ar-Rahman, Ar-Raheem, As-Salam.*
Peace and only Peace is my nature and my name,
And this is what I say:

"There is no shameful punishment
For those who disbelieve or doubt,
There is no painful retribution
For those who cannot see or wish more proof.
Each mind has lived a different life,
Each body lived a different place,
Their view of what's in front of them
Can hardly be the same.
It's the good deeds that God looks for,
The arms held out to help,
The smile that greets a passer-by,
The waving of one's hands,
The good words said in greeting,
The tears shed for another,
The goodwill offered tirelessly,
And the laughter with a friend.

"At the end of two lives lived,
Though different they may be,
At the approach to the Great Realm,
At the entrance of a Gate,
God does not check what they believe,
God does not ask what land they're from,
He watches out for simpler things,
Gestures without words,
He waits for telling signs
Like courtesy and grace,
Or if they're walking hand in hand.
To them their salutation will be 'peace'.

"Have we ever asked
How the Parent of 'all' men
Could ask a son to kill another,
To kill another son?
He never would, He never could,
On this can't we agree?
Instead save lives for Him,
Tell men to put their weapons down,
Tell them not to fight,
Tell them not to aim and shoot,
Not to give men wounds.

"Say, learn to discard fear,
Learn to hold your anger back,
Hold out your hand for him to reach
And lift your brother up.
Show him love and kindness,
Show him kindly peace,
For God is not a God of war
And God is not a God of hate,
He is and always will contain
Peace, peace and only peace.
So let me say what I believe,
We dishonour what He is,
Say, He never will encourage hate,
We betray Him when we fight,
We flay Him when we kill.
God is a God of love,
God is a God of peace,
We may worship Him profoundly,

But our love also belongs and should be given
To the whole of humankind.

"And let us ask of those
Who speak of a Great Satan.
Is he the doctors and the nurses
Who've pledged their lives to humankind,
Whose Hippocratic Oath
Is a cornerstone of their lives,
Where 'whoever' may be sick
Lies in their caring arms?

"Ask, who is this said Great Satan
Who looms dark in some minds?
Is he all the children
Playing in the parks,
Is he all the millions
Who live and march for peace,
Or is he all the writers
Whose words read only peace?

"Ask, what is this said Great Satan
Who barks and yowls and snaps?
The common folk who work two jobs
Just to make ends meet,
The millions who send charity
To 'whoever' is in need,
Or perhaps those of the Scripture
Who stand up for what's right?

"Let's not judge the great whole
By the actions of a few,
To generalise is misleading,
Can lead to great untruth,
And to teach a partial truth
Maintains great ignorance,
And a people who are ignorant
Are easily misled.

"I dwell with you in gladness,
With pride I gladly do,
Brothers full of peacefulness,
With peace towards Mankind,
Refusing to be swayed
To hatred and contempt,
Never rallying with warmongers
Under banners that defile,
But holding fast to the middle way,
To peace and glad acceptance
Of other peoples' ways.

"If your voice is raised in peace,
In peace instead of war
With warmth within your heart,
With purity of soul,
I repeat it is with greatest pride,
That I willingly do abide
Steadfastly in your core,
Steadfastly at your side.

"Ask, is there really need
To lose a hundred million more,
Suffer a hundred million losses,
Hear a hundred million screams,
Shed a hundred million tears,
Over a hundred million deaths,
For whom the bells might never cease,
To toll through endless nights,
And truth will never cease to shame?
For never have so many
Been put in such grave risk
By the ambition, fear or delusion,
The false guidance of so few.

"I add my voice to those who say
God's world is a land of many, living side by side
Who believe in peace and tolerance,
Are blind to colour and race,
Who look at each and every faith
With moderation and respect,
Who are loyal to the well-being
Of each and every man,
That leaves each man at ease
To share this common world
As a common human band
With commonwealth humanity
Across God's many lands.

"This is what I wish to say,
The message I wish to give,

And to whom do I wish these words to reach,
Whom shall my thoughts address?

"Sand, dwellers there within,
Walking tall and straight,
Who wash their feet, their hands, their face,
Who purify before they pray,
Prostrate down low before the One they love.

"Those who sit in rows of pews,
Those who sing their holy songs,
Who kneel before the Altar,
Who bow before the Cross,
Who take the bread and wine
Of the One they love.

"To those who unroll scrolls,
Those who curl their hair,
Who congregate before the Ark,
Interwoven as the vine,
Who pray in private under shawls,
Sing blessings to the One they love.

"To you I give these words,
You that God so cherishes:
Despite our vast inadequacies
He clearly sees your sacrifices,
Despite our past atrocities,
He clearly sees your offerings.

"I call for peace, yet even so
I'm worried when I read the Books.
I ask, use only half the contents
And put aside the rest:
If I could, if I were there, I'd do just this,
Amend the Books, remove distress,
Abridge and cut, sever then shed,
Teach only that which helps,
Ignore verses that cause unrest,
Use only that which stands the test,
That is summarized quite simply as
Goodwill to 'all' men, and peace on Earth.
Bear with me my brothers,
This is my belief.

"There no compulsion in religion,
Yet still there are those who do.
There no compulsion in religion,
God inspired us not to do.
There no compulsion in religion,
Yet these words are said and forgotten
Within one breath,
Exhaled without a thought,
Uttered without commitment, without force.

"Indeed, there is no compulsion,
No-one should be coerced,
Love is the only *Caliph*,
No one man on earth,
Peace is God's only doctrine

And the peaceful are with Him.
With peace there's no coercion
For peace will lead to peace,
And peace is the only Faith,
Have faith in God, in Allah, in peace.

"And understand that righteousness
Does not give the right,
Does not give the license,
To end another's life.
Understand the other
Lives because of God,
Understand the other
Is there for our salvation.
It is God who gives him back his life
Each morning when he wakes,
It is not for us to make that day
The day he meets his death.

"Understand that when God put
The blood within our veins,
He put the blood within his too
And put it there to stay,
Not to drain away, into the soil beneath,
Not to be displaced, by bullet or by blade,
But to flow strong through his heart
Until a later date,
To surge each minute and each hour
Until his natural dying day.

"And be careful when you use your Book
To scorn another person,
For another may open his and scorn
Quite rightly in return.
Better still to compare and share,
For if truth be known,
Most know little of the others' Scriptures,
And how can you know the whole
By staring at just one Book,
At just one brick, blinkered,
Fixated on just one tome?
And if truth again be known,
How often have we said
We know but a tiny portion of our God,
For all is not disclosed,
Far more is still left hidden,
So far more is to be said?

"There is no 'them' and 'us',
There is no 'us' and 'them',
There is only family,
There is only 'We',
There is only One World,
There is only Earth.
It's home to all God's nations
And home to all God's tribes,
The strong are there to help the weak,
Not to bleed them dry,
And if you hear another cry
Go and find out why.

"The surface of the globe
Is our common floor,
The sky above our heads
Is our common roof.
Walk and talk and smile and laugh
In Common Humanity,
Extend our minds beyond our own,
Live for others' sakes,
For humility requires
Removal of the self,
And belief in God requires
We widen paths to peace.
This is how I see things,
This is my belief."

The next surprise to meet
The Reverend as he woke
Were the eyes that watched him curiously
In a comfortable *majlis*,
Where light streamed through the window
And brightened up the space,
Where he squinted for a while
As it shone upon his face,
And felt he had to offer
An apology of sorts.

"I hope I did not shock you,
My name is Reverend Smith.
A visitor sometimes comes inside me,
Comes and goes as he sees fit,
Says things as he sees them,
Offers his beliefs.
His name is Peace and he's from the East,
From a land of the *Qu'ran*,
I'm slowly learning who he is
And see him sometimes with his darkened tan.
I don't know what he said today,
For him I left my body,
But I hope you will consider his words
For they don't mean to offend.
Thank you for taking care of me,
For waiting at my side,
And if you have any questions, I'll do my best,
But you are the proponents of your Belief,
And he was born in your religion, not mine,

He must be eager to talk to you,
To say what's on his mind."

His hosts wore differing gowns,
Three different demeanours and frowns,
They turned and whispered close to ear,
One stroked his handsome beard.
Their skin was smooth,
Their perfume strong,
Their clothes were spick and span,
One was the Imam of the mosque
Who had used his Friday voice, who said,
"We welcome you with courtesy,
You are a teacher of the Book,
But you will admit your presence today
Was somewhat unforeseen
Except by Allah who has written all
And Allah knows what's best,
And what's best for us is orthodox,
On what all of us agree,
On consensus of our scholars,
And in light of what was spoken today,
You 'visitor' is estranged,
And we wonder to your well-being,
Please, consider seeing a doctor,
You may be coming unhinged.

"We can't allow such teaching,
We can't permit a change
Or any innovation in what is written,

In the core of our Belief.
We do believe in dialogue,
Dialogue's well and good,
But our ears will only hear so much
And won't hear any more.
You we can forgive
For you're ignorant of our ways,
And you're welcome to return
To learn more about our truth,
And we wish you well, however advise
You seek out the Sufis,
For their ways are bent on being awry
And, respectfully as we see things,
This will do you more good."


He left the dome of the impressive Mosque,
Walked to the park Boathouse,
He bought a latte,
Took a terrace table
And looked across the water.
He wondered what the visitor had said,
On the imprint that it left,
But one thing for sure, the Imam was
Definitely not impressed,
And reminded him of the Bishop
Who had fretted and admonished.
The water was so peaceful,
Its sparkles soothed and calmed,
But deep in thought he felt detached,
Was neither here nor there.

He nestled in the ambiance
Of nature mixed by man
Until a figure came up to him
To introduce himself.

"Excuse me sir," he said.
"My name is Sulaiman,
I saw and heard you in the Mosque,
Before being chaperoned off.
The words you said intrigued me
For some I'd heard before
In the quietness of private thought
Between obligatory prayers.
But private thought is well and good
As long as it's not said,
As long as what's said doesn't question
What theology demands is truth
To keep society cohesive,
To keep the faithful loyal,
Along with deeply rooted traditions
And deeply guarded mores,
In fact you said what I could have,
But didn't to keep the peace,
But by saying nothing and changing nothing
Do I delay the chance for peace?"

The Reverend was uplifted
To have an ear that listened,
That allowed him to talk freely,
That thankfully permitted the possibility

That he wasn't so deranged,
So he completed introductions.
"It really is my pleasure,
I fully understand,
When prudence asks for silence,
When prudence asks to stay one's words
When an ear is not quite ready,
But Peace has come and talks through me
So perhaps the time is pertinent,
For to deny Peace his voice
Perhaps is to deny peace on Earth
And that's the crux of the matter."

The Reverend continued explaining
All that had recently happened
And Sulaiman continued expounding on
The origin of the verses,
Each *sura* and each *aya*
That had been added to
And each could see a logic
In the purpose of the words.
And friendship blossomed quickly
Through this common cause,
And evident was that friendship
Was an important part of peace,
And building and maintaining friendship
Was the very root of peace,

"You know," continued Sulaiman.
"Our Books have never changed,

But Books can be interpreted
In many different ways,
Our Books are supposed to lead to peace,
But also lead to war,
They're supposed to keep us on the straight path,
But I believe also lead astray,
And the greatest stories ever told
Can be the greatest cons
Depending on the politics and emotions of
The one who reads aloud:
Does he intend to sooth with balm
Or pull a holy trigger?
Does lamb's wool keep us warm at night
Or fall across our eyes?
And does love extend across all borders
Or is death extolled instead?
Some of us don't think when learning,
Some don't think by choice,
But the net result is a world in danger
Of falling off a cliff,
And truth sometimes can defy common sense,
And where's the common sense it that?
If they can be abrogated even once,
They can be abrogated again,
And over a thousand of years of adherence
That's a lot of missed abrogations.
Revisions are in order,
Amendments should be made,
That leave no ambiguity but seeing
Others as equals to be loved.

At times I find I'm imagining
A different world to ours,
A world of simple axioms
To which every man adheres,
At least that's what I believe,
But would be ostracised for voicing.

"In reading all our Books
I often see the way of love,
But then again I'm quite alarmed
At what can be instructed
To men who don't see context
Except the context of their own.
I see the Old and New Testaments
Sitting side by side
As if the Bible's progression to peace
Has been reversed, turned upside down.
Though we're taking one step forward
We're taking two steps back,
One page it is forgiveness,
The next it is revenge.
Am I a man within a religion?
Whose duty lies in honesty,
But in the midst of religious men
For whom such reasoning is treason?
Aren't I in the Western Worldif I were
Of Christian peace and forgiveness,
Yet astride a lingering meridian
Of military might and self-interest?
I can and do submit

To Allah's love and peace,
But find a great impediment
In our Holy Books themselves
Which can be read by peaceful men
To build a world of peace,
That can be read by resentful men
And fill the world with hate.

"We don't believe that God was man,
Don't teach the Crucifixion,
But I sometimes enter churches
And have listened to your hymns
And feel we're throwing out the baby
With the holy bath water,
For the message of peace and love
Is evidently paramount.
But please don't be mislead
By voices selling papers,
For the same message and understanding
Is taught by peaceful minds in *masjids*
All around the world.
Both you and I have Holy Nights
Where the stars are shining brightly,
Let's put our heads together
So our hearts might bind sincerely."
The two exchanged their details,
They'd meet again most likely.

\*\*\*\*\*

The following morning the telephone rang,
Again it was the Bishop,
Who gave him one last warning
About tomorrow's Sunday sermon,
A reminder what his job entailed,
Why he received his salary,
That no-one was indispensable,
That services could be dispensed with
If sermons weren't delineated.
This didn't help the Reverend,
Whose life was being questioned,
For he was still between the Doctrine
And the insistent voice of Peace,
But he had a few small errands to run
So he walked down into town
Along the narrow High Street,
Into Saturday's gentle bustle,
But though he smiled and greeted
Townsfolk he'd known for years,
Faces turned away from him
And whispers drenched the traffic noise,
So instead he took the car
And drove outside his valley
To the nearest larger conurbation
Where his face was hardly known.

His shopping list was short,
Was only a matter of minutes,
But it got forgotten in his pocket
By the weight of other pounding thoughts,

By the push and pull of argument,
Of juxtapositioning points of view
And endless, spiralling counterarguments
That counter jabbed and poised.
Locked within this maelstrom
He became a little giddy
So took a seat and took a breath
So he wouldn't feel so dizzy,
And closed his eyes to stave commotion
Of shoppers pounding pavements
Till time had passed and panic lessened,
And thoughts began to order,
And songs began to reappear
Inside this music lover:
'At night he spoke to me,
A phantom in my mind,
Wishing you were somehow here,
In dreams my companion came.'
And much loved hymns began to cheer
The mind of this good Christian:
'Lord and Father of Mankind
Forgive our foolish ways,
Re-clothe us in our rightful minds,
In purer lives thy service find,
In deeper reverence praise,
In deeper reverence praise.'

But, the question came,
How far was one to revere?
How much reverence to be paid?

Was God so needy of such praise,
Such ardent adulation,
While his children all around the world
Were suffering in their millions?
Was time spent down upon one's knees
In fervent adoration,
Time that could be spent in others' homes
Fixing what was broken?
*'Bismillah, Al-Rahman, Al-Raheem,*
*Al-Hamdu lillah Rabil-Alamein,*
*Ah-Rahman, Ah-Raheem,*
*Maliki Yaumid-Deen.'*
But, the question came,
For a God of love and a God of peace
Why was He insistent
On planning doom, a Day of Judgement,
A burning Day to end existence?
And so the Reverend knew, for all that he had learnt,
He still had much to understand,
Much more to ascertain,
Much more for him to question,
Answers to be found,
And he looked again with eyes reopening
Along the bustling street
And saw the visitor on a corner
Beckoning him to his feet.

Peace took him down a side street
Then along an alleyway
Which opened to a pleasant park,

A common chapel field.
Peace walked along the eastern edge
In and out of shadows
Of buildings built around the square
Till he stopped before some windows.
The Reverend was surprised
For the windows stained and bright
Held symbols of all religions
And were as such unique.
And more surprised he was
To read the sign above the door
For Peace had brought him to the threshold
Of a Spiritualist church,
The Church belittled by the Bishop,
Frowned on by even him,
Thought to be at least eccentric,
Held to be skewwhiff,
But Peace walked on in through the door
Ushering in the Reverend
Till the usher of the church itself
Sat the Reverend down,
And as the good man looked about
At the growing congregation
He soon found he was left alone,
The visitor was not around.

And then the service started
And expectant voices hushed,
And the platform filled with several folk
To perform a given task,

With a simple board above their heads
Saying 'God is Peace and God is Love'.
One was a cheerful chairwoman,
She greeted everyone
And introduced the order of service
And the visiting medium.
Another read a reading
He had written for the day,
And another led the congregation
In prayer in their own way,
And everyone sang a song or two
Much like his very own flock,
And then the medium stood
To give an opening address
That seemed neither to be rehearsed nor written,
Yet flowed and made good sense.

Then she closed her eyes,
And then she opened them,
Then she pointed to a woman
To give her Richard's name,
To give his age and character,
To describe his looks in detail,
To talk with great compassion
About her son who'd taken his life.
'He's sorry mum, he knows you hurt,
But he couldn't carry on,
When Judy left he fell to pieces,
He had nothing left to live for.
Please understand, he's getting help

From loved one's all around him,
He's in good hands, he'll be all right,
He's still alive, but with the dear departed.'
The woman fell to crying, uncontrollably,
Her daughter held her hands
And comforted her in grief
While the medium explained that life didn't end
The moment after death,
That her job was to prove that only bodies die,
That the spirit is eternal, that loved ones still survive.
And in a similar fashion
She pointing out to others,
She continued giving evidence
With names and dates and facts,
With proofs, events and evidence
That she couldn't possibly guess.
Sometimes she brought laughter,
Sometimes she brought tears,
And sometimes she expounded views
Of the Spiritualist Church,
That God is God and also
All spirits good in the world beyond
Who never ever stopped loving
Those they left on Earth.

The Reverend was resistant,
But the same he was impressed,
He remained inherently sceptical,
Though couldn't deny the medium's words
Accepted by the recipients

Of the messages she gave:
It seemed neither trick nor guesswork,
Her tongue was quite specific.
And then her eyes fell on to his
And she frowned unlike before:
She seemed at odds with what was now
Entering her mind.
"May I come to you," she said, "My light is over you,
But I must admit this spirit is
Something that's quite new.
I know you are a man of God,
Preach sermons of your own,
But here I have a visitor
Who says ... *asalam* ... *aleykum.*
He's caused you some concern,
Has turned things on their head,
But all the same he is a friend
And things need to be said.
He's coming close, he's from the East,
I'll do my best to mediate,
Though his ways and words be foreign,
I'll do my best to express
Exactly what is wished be uttered
For his words will soon be yours,
To transmit as you see fit,
His words will be your purpose,
Your sermons will be his." And she began:

"The world that God foresees,
The world that He has planned,

Is rich in its diversity,
Not barren desert sand.
It's richer for its differences,
Richer for its tribes,
It would be far, far poorer
If oppressed and centralised.

"Books are not just Books
You can open at a certain page
And find excuse to war,
The liberty to hate.
God has nought to do with this,
How could He, ask yourself.
He is not a tyrant,
He is not insane,
It is not His Will
To see His children killed.
So do not cry His name
In the name of what's inhumane,
When the very essence of His being
Is the path to living peace.

"He does not wish we use a Book
To crush another down,
And does not wish emotion
To remove our peaceful minds.
And as these words are given
They form a Constitution
For peaceful coexistence,
For peaceful folk who live in peace

Understand the beliefs of others,
And welcome others' speech.
This is what he says,
This is what he believes.

"Differences are plain to see
And plain to understand,
The parting into different streams
That all end at a strand,
But a difference is a difference,
Not a cause for war,
Not to cause millennia
Of enmity and strife,
But to be accepted
In goodwill and in peace.

"Do not think it bothers God
That a difference may occur,
It is only natural, to do what one thinks right.
So, do not think your way, is the only one,
For doesn't a tree grow branches
To stretch across the Earth,
To give shade to greater numbers
From the midday glare and heat.

"Let one man walk his path
While we walk along our own,
If God, who's Love, is at our centre
We will easily know,
The paths that each have taken

Are not contentious points,
Only needs of human beings
That can be understood.
Is he that much different? Is he to be loathed?
He sheds a tear at death,
He cries with joy at birth,
He struggles through his life,
He learns with age then dies.

"Don't we do the same? Aren't we just like him?
A brother he still is,
So hold him in our hearts with love
And use the power of kindness
Not of foolish words,
And never close our door,
Never build a wall,
And never make a barrier
That can't be broken down.
Partings are only branchings,
No need for caustic lips,
They are to be expected
Without judgement or ill will,
And are to be accepted
With peace and openness.

"He is not unfaithful,
To God he gives his prayers,
One God and One Love,
This he never changed.

"Our job is to convince
The unconvincable,
Our job is to persuade
The unpersuadable,
Our job is to expound
The good from every Book,
And speak the verses dear to God
Of peace, of peace, of peace.

"The only ideology
That God could ever teach
Starts and ends with *as-salam,*
Starts and ends with peace.
The only *Caliphate*
That should be realised
Holds this as the truth,
Maintains this simple end.
Love is the only Kingdom,
Where many standards fly,
Where the flags of all God's nations
Flutter side by side,
A spectacle of colour
A sight to bring God joy,
Knowing that His children
Abide with Him in peace.

"Its leaders are His servants
Renouncing harm and ill,
His servants are the peacemakers
Who speak and live in peace,

Whose hearts are warm with peace,
Whose minds are set on peace.
For God's Kingdom doesn't stop
At a nation's walls,
God's Kingdom will allow each man
To walk in any street,
In any town around the world
In security and safely, in happiness and peace.

"A man may walk before a mosque,
Or walk before a church,
Walk before a synagogue,
A temple or a shrine,
And know that in each dwells
A welcome and goodwill,
Food when he is hungry,
Water for his thirst.
This is what he says,
This is his belief.

"The final brick was placed,
But the mortar was not mixed,
What holds the bricks together
Was often overlooked.
The mortar's as important
As each brick upon each brick:
Too strong and it will crack,
Too loose and it won't stick,
It needs to be quite flexible
To allow for tests of faith.

"When trembles come,
When opinions shift,
The mortar should allow
For expansion and contraction,
For generations' ebbs and flows.
It will stop the bricks from grinding,
Keep the Mansion standing,
To lie peaceful with the seasons,
Leaving ample room for reason,
To settle with the times.

"And remember that a brick
Can be viewed from all six sides
And each side can look different
Though each is just as wide,
Don't stand too close,
You'll see much less,
Step back and see much more,
For a brick is only one
Of a thousand more around,
And a man who stands too near
Will limit his perspective:
By moving back a small amount,
He'll have a wider outlook.

"Do not let our focus
Fix on just one piece,
Look to the left and to the right
Then look up and down.
Step back even further,

Visit different lands,
And we will see God's Mansion
Is far grander than believed.
Its shape is yet unknown to all,
It has colours never seen,
It has many nooks and crannies
And chambers long and tall.
Go inside and see them all
Before we know the whole.

"The mortar's there to bind,
To fill the gaps between,
To unify and keep together
The home of all Mankind.
The final brick's been put in place
But the Mansion's incomplete,
And it will remain unfinished
Until the family of Man
Stops killing in the streets.

"It is with a parental heart that God does see,
A parental heart that God does feel,
A parental heart that God does judge,
A parental heart that God does give,
Needless to say, it is the heart of Love,
A heart without malice, a heart without greed,
No hate, no rage,
A selfless heart that forms decisions,
That continues loving across all regions.
For each person born is God's child,

Each person born is just a child,
Life is short, life can be hard,
But God wishes love, and wishes peace,
With a heart of pity, a heart that's big,
He encompasses the globe, with outstretched arms.

"It is warmth He brings on the coldest day,
It is light He gives in the darkest night.
The weaponry we carry, put it down,
Put it down to rust away,
Or melt into useful tools,
And do not ask permission
To take another's life,
That is God's child you're talking of,
You do not have His blessing,
You do not have the right!
This is what he says,
This is his belief.

"To mend this stricken world,
Rub balm in wounds instead of salt,
Perceive the other's scars,
His ghosts that do torment,
And say an unexpected word
Of thanks, of gratitude, of hope,
Of sorrow shared, not heaped,
Instead of unbridled hate.

"To hear the chink of metal,
Of weapon laid upon the ground,

If there is even one, there can be two.
When even one unwanted word is held in check
And nought is said instead,
When even one stone is left unthrown,
One rifle left unaimed,
The road is clearer ahead.

"This task is not beyond our means,
It's more real than just a dream,
To put a thought inside a head, where
The unimaginable normalcy of war
Can become an imaginable peace.

"A cross is just a symbol
As is the crescent moon,
Paths to peace may differ,
But to God it is the same.
He does not quibble over
Who is right and wrong,
This is a preoccupation
For those with narrow minds.

"Let Him hear talk of bridges,
Let Him see respect,
Let Him see His nations,
Bid goodwill and bid peace,
Let Him hear A*l-Fatiha*
And also the Lord's Prayer,
And do not take offence
At these words you hear,

Their purpose is a single thing,
It's peace, it's peace, it's peace.
Do not react with ire,
Do not dismiss these verses,
Hear them with an open mind,
And with a peaceful heart.

"Do not let these verses
Be a cause for anger
For that it human weakness
Within the human self.
Do not tussle, do not fight,
To disagree is within one's rights,
But hear them to help bring peace to Earth
And peace to God,
For God continues suffering
And wants to feel our joy.
This is what he says,
This is his belief,
And now he leaves."

The service went beyond its hour,
But the medium filled her task,
She spoke the words that Peace had given,
She spoke until he left.
And then she also faltered,
Slumped upon her chair
Exhausted and depleted
By the energy that she'd spent,
Energy not of this world,
Far greater and far purer,
It took its toll in bodily strength,
It left her almost snoozing.

She said a word of apology,
And left her final speech
To the chairwoman filling up her water glass
Who thanked her in her niche,
Who read the notices, the healing times,
Invited all to stay, to mingle with each other,
In the adjoining anteroom.
The final song was sung
A favourite of the Reverend's,
A piece by Rutter, to bless us and to keep us,
To shine His face upon us,
To bring us peace, Amen, Ameen,
And though on unfamiliar ground
The Reverend couldn't disagree.

Intrigued the Reverend lingered,
A new face in the crowd,

He knew he would be welcomed,
It was a friendly house.
He saw the grieving mother
Whose tears now held more joy:
The service had brought comfort
Wasn't that his job too?
He saw the chairperson circulate,
Approached her when he could,
And asked about the medium
Who hadn't yet emerged,
Who nestled on the platform
Still gathering her strength.
Yet even so she'd asked for him,
Had something more to add,
For Peace had left a residue
After relinquishing his grasp.

"My boy," she said with weary breath,
"That really was unusual,
Most often I give messages
From the recently deceased.
I hear them and I see them
In my mind's ear and eye,
I often know their names and addresses,
Know how they passed away,
And convey as much as I am able
To prove they're still alive.
But your friend was greatly different,
He came from somewhere higher,
And while with me he uplifted,

And Earth seemed far, far lower,
He deeply, profoundly moved me,
And then he let me go,
But his presence lingers on,
His essence has effects,
His words were not for relatives,
But everyone on Earth.
His mission needs a voice down here,
He cannot speak without your help,
I feel he's close to God,
As close perhaps as one can get,
For God is peace and God is love,
And love and peace are God.

"I have my role in life
That comforts those distressed,
You have a role in life
To bring the world to peace.
You are a bridge between two faiths
That often clash and squabble,
Two worlds that hold the precondition
That the fault lies with the other,
Where mindsets lie embedded
That the other should be conquered.
Your role is to explain
The reasons for the troubles,
Your role's to find solutions,
Not offer endless excuses,
To endless disagreements,
To ceaseless arguments,

And just to prove that I'm not lying,
Your name is Reverend Smith!

"I'm glad I met your friend,
I'm sorry that he's gone,
But my body wasn't strong enough
To hold him for too long.
I wish you well, I wish success,
I wish you all things good,
I think you know your challenges
Have started and are just,
For peace is not a dream, it is a state of being,
Peace is there to be reclaimed,
To be initiated and believed."

\*\*\*\*\*

His wife's hair felt so soft
As he ran his fingers through it,
As he lay awake beside her
In the darkness of midnight.
He'd told her everything
That had happened on that day,
He told her that tomorrow
Might be his final Sunday.
But she kissed him unperturbed
And he marveled at her faith,
Her faith in marriage and in him,
That let her soundly sleep.

He listened to her breathing,
The miracle of life,
He warmed against her earthly flesh,
Was calmed by her unruffled soul,
Heard lines that would commence his sermon
And knew that more would follow,
Heard lines for other sermons
And saw a path unfolding,
And knew that empty mindedness
Made room for inspirations
Allowed filling to a mindfulness
That fulfilled and gave direction,
Allowed recognising preconceptions,
Conceiving new perceptions,
Allowed admitting imperfections
In what was otherwise perfected,
Allowed questioning the unquestionable
And the evolution of thought.

Before his hallowed, hollow hall, he and Peace both spoke:

"Patience is a virtue,
Patience is a need,
It is something vital
That must be taught and learnt.
It's easier with your own child
When he is young and sweet,
It's easier when your own child
Is growing through his youth,
And it's easier for your own child

When he's turned into a man,
For parents know this man
Will always be their child.
And as the man grows older
He sees the child within,
And no man lives quite long enough
To be anything but a child.
So set your expectations
At levels that are apt,
Accept his limitations
And praise his acts of peace,
For a young body carries youth so well,
But doesn't suit old age,
And old age carries wisdoms
Not yet learned in youth.

"Do not let our mind
Misguide us from a fact,
For sometimes what we think is patience
Is just the opposite:
It's a struggle deep within ourself
To suppress a lack of it.
The difference is the feeling
For patience is pure love,
Is why the peace in religion asks
To turn the other cheek,
And why the wisest live
With befitting tolerance
To create and nurture peace,
Accepting, understanding,

That when another prays,
Prays his way in peace,
God still hears his every word,
Still sees every tear.

"But if we feel frustration,
If anger grows instead,
This is a sign of straining
To contain our deficit.
But at least control is better
Than the horrors that arise
From impatience and intolerance
From bigotry and lies.
So, for the challenges that remain
Sit down in peace to talk,
But if the need arises
Step out from the room,
To calm our hearts, to calm ourselves,
To reconnect to love and wisdom,
To reconnect to peace,
To the oldest and the wisest,
Yes God, our God, who is love, who is peace.

"Who can be a servant:
A Christian or a Muslim,
A Buddhist draped in Zen,
A Hindu or a Jain,
A carpenter, a tailor, a chauffeur, a sailor,
An employer or employee,
A worker or a boss?

"A servant can be Eastern
Or Western, Asian or Arab,
European or Columbian, African or Chinese,
Bearded or clean-shaven, black or white or pink,
Smelling of *oud* or the sweat of the field,
Or dirt or coal dust or Eau-de-Cologne.
He can be tall or he can be short,
Young or old, a father or a son
A teacher or a friend, a soldier tired of war,
A husband or a bachelor,
And he can be a she, and be more than a he.

"How can we know and how can we agree?
For his voice may be loud or it may be soft,
There may be no trumpets to herald his cart,
He may point out errors
Which cannot be conceived,
Reveal for us our prejudices
And ingrained animosities,
Teach the opposite, perhaps,
To that which we believe.
He may come in winter, or summer or spring,
Perhaps in the morning, afternoon or evening,
Under the sun or under the moon and stars.
There probably won't be a banner to point him out,
And his accent may be exceptionally strange.
He may pray standing or kneeling or prostrate,
Or in quiet reflection throughout the day.
Who are those, the servants?
How can we know? How can we agree?

"We should be prepared for anyone and anything,
For what would a servant be enjoined to do?
He will plead for forgiveness instead of hate,
Implore reconciliation instead of revenge,
He will point out hypocrisy,
Discrimination and bigotry,
Deplore cruelty and demand common bonds,
Bow down in all humility before that which is love,
Never put himself higher than any other,
Help each and everyone find
The servant within one's self,
Turning 'he' into 'We' and 'them' into 'Us',
He will cry for peace and only peace,
He will never call for war,
Knowing that across every border,
Our other brothers live.
And despite his imperfections and weaknesses,
The human mistakes he will undoubtedly make,
He will strive and he will bring
All nations to agree,
On the inviolability of life
And to an inviolable peace.


"Do not let our bricks, be the ones that fill
The only hole that yet remains
Above the window sill.
Leave room to look outside,
Don't block ourselves within,
For so much more lies out there
Don't lock ourselves right in.

Do not use our bricks
To seal the final door,
Not only will there be no way out,
But also no way in.
Do not trap God's light
And live amidst the dusk,
Leave holes to let more light in,
There's far more than we think.
And when looking at the last brick,
Don't forget the very first,
Don't even take our eye from it,
For things will turn out worse.
It is the most important,
The foundation of all hope,
That's constant and everlasting,
The centre of all life:
'Do not do to others
What we wouldn't do to self.'

"Do not condemn the servants,
They've proved themselves in peace,
They've done the things asked of them,
Gone places they've been bid.
It is for peace they speak,
They seek nothing for themselves,
And they are ones of many
Who've served the path of peace.
This servant speaks within his limits,
With a heart and soul for peace,
But if another hears me also,

Then add more to this verse.
For there is nothing in these verses
That intends anything but peace,
So accept them with an open heart
And end God's suffering.

"To whom are these words given?
To Christians and to Jews,
To Muslims and to all,
And even to the servants
Who are human too,
That no-one moves too far astray
That no-one strays too far,
That all may keep their self-control,
That all may keep their calm.
To those that pray in earnest,
That they may listen too,
For God speaks as well as listens,
That they may hear His voice.
To those with no religion
Yet still have ears to hear,
Who wish to live in peace
Which is God's greatest Will.
To those who suffer foolish men
Bedecked with foolish aims,
To those who've never really questioned
Why they carry guns,
To those who've never really questioned
Why they kill God's sons.
To enemies far too proud

To admit how much they fear,
When fear itself can disappear
When living by these words.

"Life and death has shown me,
That salvation's guaranteed
Through goodwill to Mankind,
That service to all men
Will keep the Earth alive,
That the future of humanity
Lies squarely in Man's hands.
For God is love and God is peace,
Our God is love, our God is peace,
And I bear witness that God is only love,
That God is only peace,
I bear witness that religion is a Way of love,
That religion is a Way of peace.
So come in peace to peace,
Live with your neighbour in peace,
And invite your enemy to peace,
For God is love and God is peace.
No God except the God of love,
No Way except the Way of peace.
This is how I see things,
This is my belief,
For I believe that God is peace,
And I believe He wills for peace,
And I believe there will be peace."

*****

His sermon went quite well
Considering the empty nave,
He'd ventured into concepts
Beyond the pastoral pale,
And though the bells had failed to ring,
And though the pews had ostracized,
He'd delivered what he knew to be
A homily to Belief revolutionised.

He thought the church was empty,
With the exception of his wife,
This day even Doubt had let him be
And the mice may even have gone on strike,
But as he made towards the door
Two figures stepped out from the columns
And greeted him with friendly smiles,
Two smiles that did so gladden him:
Michael the hermit walked on up,
Winked and stood beside him,
Then Sulaiman approached with grace
And held his hand for shaking.
There stood a trinity of human beings,
With a good wife added on,
A trinity of unlikeliness,
Of burgeoning unorthodoxy,
A trinity of diversity, a trinity of four,
With learning as their goal.

Their debate was to begin,
Their ears were there to hear,

Their discussions were a dialogue
In which no-one was unheard,
Where each had something fresh to add,
Bound by friendship and respect,
They'd continue to communicate,
Bound by common good.
They'd construct a greater whole,
And though Peace was no longer in their midst
Peace was still there all the same,
For in each one Peace had made a foothold,
And peace and only peace
Was the only aim.

## THE END

## Glossary

| | |
|---|---|
| *Al-Adhan* | call to prayer |
| *Al-Fatiha* | first chapter of the Qu'ran |
| *As-salam aleykum* | peace be on you (greeting) |
| *(Wa) aleykum salam* | (and) to you be peace |
| *Aya* | verse (of Qu'ran) |
| *Gutra* | male head scarf |
| *Insha'Allah* | God willing |
| *Iqama* | second (shorter) call to prayer |
| *Ismi Salam* | my name is Peace |
| *Jumaa* | Friday prayer |
| *Masha'Allah* | thanks be to God |
| *Majlis* | gathering room |
| *Masjid* | mosque |
| *Oud* | woody perfume |
| *Suraat* | chapters (of Qu'ran) |
| *Thobe* | long male robe |

*Bismillah, Ah-Rahman, Ah-Raheem,* (recited at the beginning of most suraat) *Al-Hamdu lillah Rabil-Alamein, Ah-Rahman, Ah-Raheem, Maliki Yaumid-Deen* ... (the beginning of Al-Fatiha)

In the name of Allah, the most Compassionate, the most Merciful, all praise to Allah, the Lord of all Worlds, the most Compassionate, the most Merciful, King of the Day of Judgement ...

## The prism

The human heart is made of flesh,
Pumps blood around all limbs,
But also it is made of glass,
For it is too a prism
That can lead to joy and freedom,
But, that can be a prison.
Shine love upon its surface
And a rainbow you will see
That is bright and joyful to the eye,
For in it you will view
Compassion, truth and honesty,
Forgiveness, hope and peace,
All the things that show
The presence of its God,
The God of love, of peace.
But pour hate upon its plane
And the arch that you will see
Is dark and fearful to the eye,
For in it you will view
Revenge, deceit and violence,
Despair and ignorance,
All the things that show
That God's let nowhere near,
That despite His fervent wish,
Despite His fervent hope,
The human heart decided
To turn its back on Him,
On love and peace.

## Discoveries

With or without resort to prayer,
With or without heads bowed to the ground,
The greatest minds the world has known,
Have channelled knowledge down.

With or without a pious lifestyle,
With or without a Holy Book,
They have yet discovered,
Known where it was to look.

God chooses who He wishes,
He speaks through who He can,
Persons who are closest,
To understanding Him and Man.

So don't judge one by the clothes he wears,
Or by the language that he speaks,
A procedure that may save your life,
May have come via his intelligence,
And his own beliefs.

## The crescents of the moon

Side by side the crescents lie,
A perfect fit to an engineering eye,
Little more than hairline fissures,
There's no design that could be bettered.
Neatly resting against each other,
Your job to piece all parts together.
The moon's not whole until it's full,
The night is dark when it's in pieces,
Is darker still when joints are fractures,
When seen as insurmountable abysses,
When cleaved by narrower perspectives,
Distorted by disruptive voices
Who forget respect, goodwill to others,
Would rather harm than mend old wounds,
Rather blame than understand,
Reject the choices made, the way of things,
Belittle routes that aren't their own.

## The prayer mat

If a man comes join you
While you bow within your prayer,
Then turns away towards his shrine
Or looks towards the sky,
Or raises up his arms,
Or prays only on his knees,
Then do not shun him harshly,
Let him pray in peace,
Indeed give him your prayer mat
That he may pray at ease,
That he may ask God's guidance,
That he may shed his tears.
His direction may be different,
His raiment may be strange,
But for God he performs his rituals,
The One and only God.

## Brethren

Before, you earned God's favour,
For you were enemies once,
But found it in yourselves
To join your hearts together,
And brethren you became.
But now the stakes are higher,
Discord is all around,
The devastation and loss of life
Go beyond all bounds.
So find it in your hearts
To bind yourselves together
And brethren you will be
In the Human Race.

## The sculptor

Do not insist
That when God told the Prophets to recite,
That He didn't also tell
The sculptor to sculpt,
The painter to paint,
The composer to compose,
And the writer to write,
The singer to sing,
And the dancer to dance.

It is true that words uplift
For they are a means to love,
A medium to His peace,
Yet so too are carved eyes,
So too music notes,
For His inspirations go
Far beyond mere words,
Beyond what can be written
In one's single Book.

## The instrument

Can you hear the instrument screech?
Its strings are pulled too tight,
The neck bends out and creaks and groans,
Struggles not to break.
The sound is quite discordant,
The musician cannot play,
But still the manufacturer proclaims
No adjustment shall be made.

Can you see the person walk
Quite robotically?
Denied his freedom to move at will
By tendons strung too taut.
But that's the way he's hampered,
Not his real design,
Denied the right to be himself
By faults within the system?

Can you see the mind, unable to create?
It's told the rules it must obey
Maintaining mediocrity.
It wants to soar, it wants to sing,
But false reason keeps it back,
It must limit what it wants to think,
Stagnate in what's permitted.

Don't expect a trumpet to be a harpsichord,
Don't expect a tom-tom drum to be a clarinet,

Each has its given sound,
Just like every man,
Whose melody is quite personal, is indeed his own.
This is how God's world should be:
An orchestra of variety,
Not a monotonous drone.
Your own string may be pulled tight,
Be suitable for you,
But do not insist that others,
Follow rigid ways.

Listen to their teachings,
Listen to their songs,
You will hear the beauty
God inspired within their minds,
The same words as your own,
Words the same as yours.
In all of them are peace,
In all of them are love,
In all of them they wish
Well to their fellow man.

The fact that you have arms and legs,
A body and a heart,
Is enough for you to comprehend
A brother visits living peace.
There is no need for symbol,
There is no need for fear,
God's Will is just compassion,
His is love and peace.

## Tomorrow?

I look down and watch a boy
Standing on the balls of his feet,
Alternating, rocking, waiting for help,
Wanting to sit, or lie, or fall,
But without any skin the pain would be worse,
Burnt off by the incendiary shell,
Projected by the parent of another child,
That cooked his meat rank and rare
And left his skin hanging bare,
Dripping from his fingertips,
With incomprehension in his eyes,
No eyelids left to blink,
In shock, without lips he cannot talk,
His muscles tell his pain.
Even the nurses cry, applying cream,
His legs and arms open so they won't touch,
He'll die, of course, a few hours after his friends
Who were picked up limp from the playing ground,
Who were scraped off school yard walls,
Childhoods over before their schooling ends.
This is today, tomorrow, will it be the same?
His name is Ahmed, by the way,
But it could be Aaron or Fehti or Mark,
Without his usual features, I almost cannot tell,
And do you see the pretty girl
Who lost her looks when she lost her face,
And the perfume that she wears
Is the stench of burning flesh?

She is Fatima, but she could be Dawn.
How long, how much longer
Must this go on?

And I look on just a little further
And watch a girl, just one of many,
She isn't shivering, she isn't cold,
Her quivering is uncontrolled,
She is in shock, sitting on a door step block,
Gazing into distance space
Through horror scorched upon her face,
That will not be erased,
Of her brother flying through the air
In bits and chunks of infant flesh,
Dissolving into bloody vapour,
Dust turning into reddened haze.
It will haunt her thoughts forever,
Never fully detach,
This purely obscene act,
Depriving her of childhood,
Too young to know the human reasons why,
But not to be so traumatized,
Not too dark to be turned white
By daily fear grown a thousand times.

It wasn't nature's calamity,
No volcano or earthquake,
It also wasn't God's Will:
It was a rocket fired by a man
Who was her father's age.

## To reconcile

When you hold your Book
Read only what is peace and love,
For though it may have been 'revealed'
God's words are often misunderstood,
Or misheard or disregarded,
Even distorted and discarded
By the ripples that I talked of,
By prejudice unseen,
By politics both hidden and unknown,
By emotions running fast,
So that what it was God tried to say
Was misheard by the ear,
Misshaped out of fear,
Even by the greatest men
The world has ever seen,
For God never gave His children land
To be taken by another.

These words can be a test,
Read them so you'll see
If the reaction in your heart and mind,
Is anything but peace.
And with historical perspective,
Can you reconcile
These words that have been given
With those from days long past?
That Man moves on in understanding,
That Man moves on in peace,

That Man becomes more Godlike,
That Man evolves to peace,
For God is love
And God is peace
And what could be God's Will
But peace and love in Man
And peace and love on Earth.

## A Covenant

The hand thought it had finished,
Had written what was wished,
But it's taken one more time this night
As the head is filled with visions.
It has no other choice
But to clench the pen that's needed
To write what needs be said,
To write what's being said.

It writes these last few words
Though it doesn't yet know why,
For today is Seven-Seven,
A day burnt in a nation,
A day of tragedy,
A day of those remembered,
A day of grief persisting,
Like too many other days prior
And too many others since.

But also let it be the Day
To recall what once was asked,
To seventy times seven and then again more
'Turn the other cheek',
To make a Covenant
On which ALL agree and keep,
That ALL will live together
Fulfilling joy and peace,
That ALL will hold together,

That no-one will accuse,
That no-one will abuse.

For wasn't there a time
When a song we used to sing
Of perfection of our love,
A vow to paths of peace?

Wasn't there an hour
When a treaty we did make
To end all wars and suffering,
When hostilities surely ceased?

Wasn't there a day
When church bells rang aloud,
When soldiers laid their weapons down,
Returning home at last?

Wasn't there a mass
With desire contained in fervent prayer
To reclothe us in our rightful minds,
To forgive our foolish ways?

And isn't there a land
We've heard of long ago,
Obliged to render hope,
In peace its glory find?

46990498R00096

Printed in Poland
by Amazon Fulfillment
Poland Sp. z o.o., Wrocław